This Book Belongs To:

Date & Grade:

SPECIAL THANKS TO OUR TEAM

This book is dedicated to every second grader with a passion for reading. The finished product would not have been possible without the commitment and dedication of an extraordinary team of individuals who share in our mission. To the following people, our undying gratitude:

- The Pickle Pie Gang
- The Ohio State University Department of Athletics
- Central Ohio Elementary School Teachers & Principals
- Current and Former OSU Student-Athlete Readers
- FUNdamental Football Camp Participants & Volunteers
- 8-Ball Shootout Participants & Volunteers
- Friends of The 2nd & 7 Foundation
- Interns from The Ohio State University
- Our Major Sponsors and Countless Individual Donors

Cover and Interior illustrations © 2008 Jason Tharp

The Hog Mollies & the Pickle Pie Party. Copyright © 2008 by The 2nd and 7 Foundation

ISBN 978-0-7575-5256-4
ISBN 978-0-7575-5363-9

Kendall/Hunt Publishing Company and The 2nd & 7 Foundation have the exclusive rights to reproduce this work, to prepare derivative works from this work, to publicly distribute this work, to publicly perform this work and to publicly display this work.

Printed in the United States of America

10 9 8 7 6 5 4 3 2 1   13 12 11 10 09 08

SECONDANDSEVEN
F O U N D A T I O N

The 2nd & 7 Foundation was developed by three former Ohio State student-athletes: Buckeye graduates Mike Vrabel, Luke Fickell, and Ryan Miller. The three were college teammates who decided to give back to the community once their days making tackles in Ohio Stadium were over.

In 2000, the foundation sponsored the inaugural FUNdamental Football Camp for young kids, and the proceeds were used to purchase books for second graders in seven Central Ohio elementary schools (thus, the creation of the foundation's name). Since that time, The 2nd & 7 Foundation has grown as its founders' passion to **"tackle illiteracy"** has increased.

The **"tackle illiteracy"** program now includes reading to second graders in classrooms all over Ohio, and provides each of the children in those classrooms with a book to take home for further enjoyment. The Ohio State University has also been involved in reaching out to the community through this program, by allowing current student-athletes to participate in the readings.

The 2nd & 7 Foundation hopes you enjoy its debut book as we bring the community together around this common goal of "tackling illiteracy."

If you would like more information about The 2nd & 7 Foundation, please visit: www.secondandseven.com.

The Hog Mollies and the Pickle Pie Party

Written by: The 2nd & 7 Foundation
Illustrated by: Jason Tharp

SECONDANDSEVEN
FOUNDATION

KENDALL/HUNT PUBLISHING COMPANY
4050 Westmark Drive   Dubuque, Iowa 52002

Harley, Sprout, Hoppy and Duke were the best of friends. Everyone called them the Hog Mollies. They were always playing and working well together.

Sprout

Hoppy

One day while playing hide and seek, Duke stumbled upon an old piece of paper in the attic. "Maybe we should ask Grandma about it," he suggested to the others.

"You found the pickle pie recipe!" Grandma exclaimed
when the Hog Mollies handed her the worn paper.
"I haven't seen that recipe since I was about your age."

"Each of my friends and I had a special job to help bake the biggest, most delicious pickle pie ever tasted—"
"PICKLE pie? That doesn't sound very tasty," interrupted Harley.

"Oh, but it is wonderful," continued Grandma. "Some of my favorite memories are from the Pickle Pie Parties we used to have. We invited everyone in town to eat and dance and sing all night long. I really miss those days."

The Hog Mollies decided to surprise Grandma and bring back the Pickle Pie Party that very day. Together they would team up to find all the ingredients. The pickle pie recipe called for:

Flour

Sugar

Eggs

Pickles

Sprout was the first to find his ingredient and quickly ran back to the kitchen.
"Pickle Pie Party tonight at Grandma's!"

On the other side of town, Harley was collecting enough sugar for the recipe. As he ran back to the kitchen, he spread the news of the party to everyone he saw, "Pickle Pie Party tonight at Grandma's!"

"But don't tell Grandma... it's a surprise!"

Hoppy decided to visit the chicken farm to get the eggs for the pickle pie. He very gently carried them all the way back to the kitchen, never dropping a single egg. When curious people asked, he explained, "Pickle Pie Party tonight at Grandma's!"

"But don't tell Grandma... it's a surprise!"

CHICKEN COOP

Sprout, Harley and Hoppy met back in the kitchen, but Duke was nowhere to be found. "I hope he gets here soon," uttered Harley. "We can't make the pickle pie without him."

A few minutes later Duke walked through the door, his head hanging low. "I looked everywhere," he said, "but I couldn't find pickles. I went from garden to garden all over town. I even went to see if Farmer Smith had grown any pickles. But I couldn't find pickles anywhere!"

"Don't worry, Duke, we've found all the other ingredients," said Sprout. "We'll help you find the pickles, too." The Hog Mollies set their ingredients down to assist Duke.

teamwork!

After a few moments of brainstorming, Hoppy had an idea. "Grandma will know where to find pickles," he said.

"But we don't want to ruin the surprise party," worried Harley.

Then the Hog Mollies all realized something. "Grandpa!" they shouted. They all remembered Grandpa bringing up jars of fruits and vegetables from the basement . . . maybe he would know.

let's ask GRANDPA!!!

Duke led the gang to Grandpa. "Do you know where pickles come from?" they asked him.

"Sure," he replied. "Come with me."

The Hog Mollies looked confused as Grandpa led them to a huge patch of cucumbers in the middle of Grandma's garden. "Here is where it all begins," he proclaimed as he plucked a perfectly ripe cucumber from its vine.

The gang just looked at each other and shrugged.
Knowing they were all still confused, Grandpa then led
them to the basement cellar.

In the basement, Grandpa threw open the cellar door.
The Hog Mollies were amazed to see jars of the most
beautiful colors arranged neatly on shelves. One whole
row was full of the brightest green they had ever seen.

"Pickles!" they yelled.
Grandpa then explained how Grandma brought him cucumbers from the garden, and with a few simple steps they became pickles.

Now that they found the final ingredient, the Hog Mollies were ready to bake their pickle pie. The gang grabbed jars of pickles and walked upstairs to the kitchen.

"Thanks for your help," Duke told the others. "It is so much fun when we work together."

One at a time, the Hog Mollies proudly added each ingredient to the mixing bowl. Finally, it was time for the Pickle Pie Party.

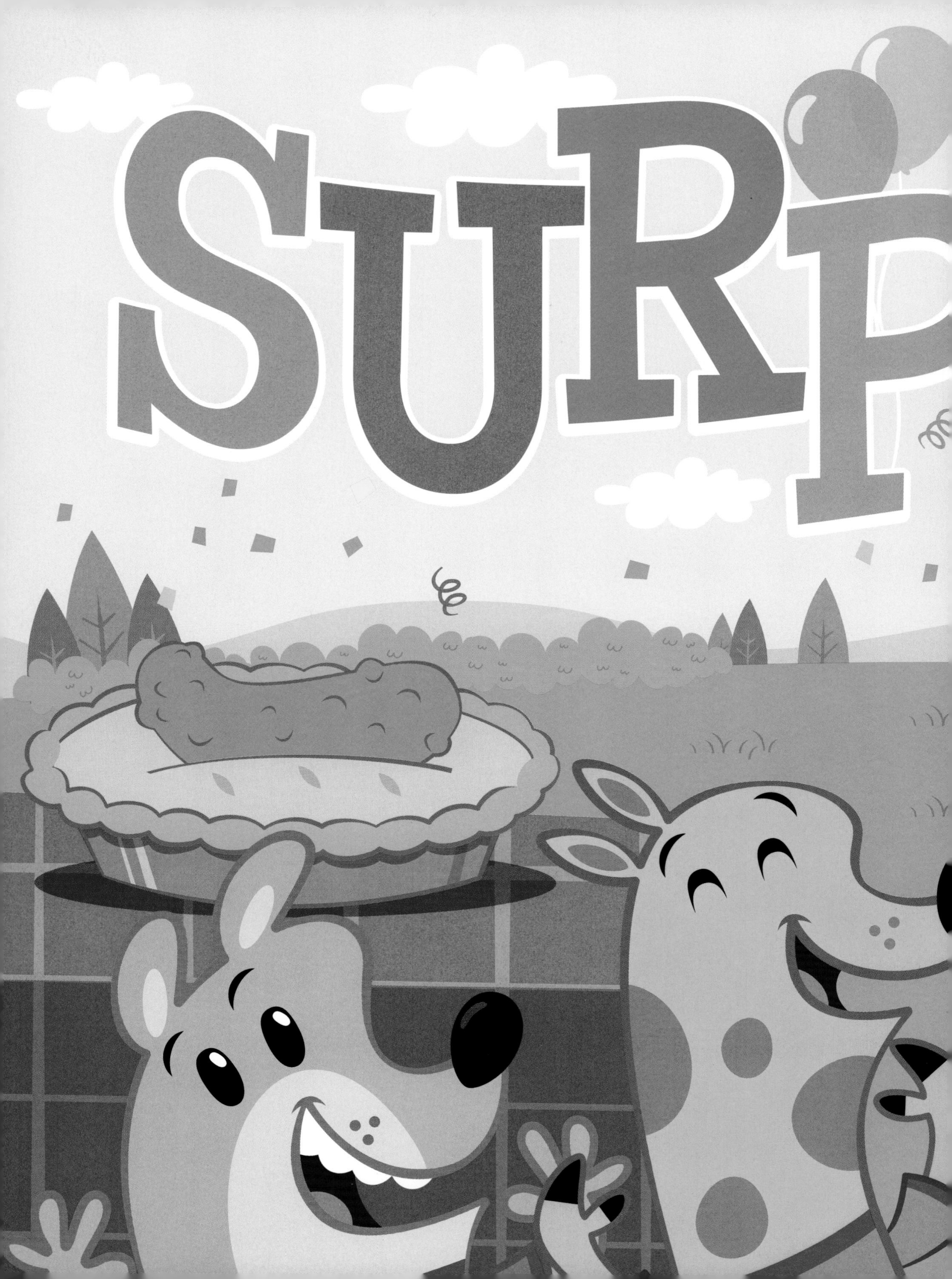
SURP

RISE!!

Everyone ate a piece of the pickle pie, danced and sang. "This Pickle Pie Party is just as good as the ones I remembered," Grandma said with a big smile on her face. "But the fact that you worked together to plan a surprise makes it the best Pickle Pie Party ever!"

How to Turn Cucumbers into Pickles

1. FIND A GROWN-UP TO HELP!

2. Wash the cucumbers.

3. Wash and sterilize jars and lids.

4. Mix vinegar and pickle spice mix and bring to a boil.

5. Fill jars with cucumbers and pickle spice mix. Then put lids on.

6. Boil the sealed jars for approximately five 5 minutes.

7. For the best flavor, wait at least two weeks to eat. Enjoy!

i used teamwork to...

_____

_____

_____

_____

_____

_____

_____

_____